The Giant from Nowhere

First published in 2018
by Jessica Kingsley Publishers
73 Collier Street
London N1 9BE, UK
and
400 Market Street, Suite 400
Philadelphia, PA 19106, USA

www.jkp.com

The accompanying PDF can be downloaded
from *www.jkp.com/voucher* using the code
KEYWYFE

Library of Congress Cataloging in Publication Data
A CIP catalog record for this book is available from the Library of Congress

British Library Cataloguing in Publication Data
A CIP catalogue record for this book is available from the British Library

ISBN 978 1 78592 535 1
eISBN 978 1 78450 928 6

Printed and bound in China

The Giant from NOWHERE

Frances Dickens

Illustrated by Peter Hudspith

Jessica Kingsley Publishers
London and Philadelphia

The Giant came from Nowhere, which is a desolate place to be,
for nobody else lived there and there was no one to talk to.
So he simply left Nowhere in order to find Somewhere, where
he might find company.

And he did find Somewhere. It was a small village in the middle of the countryside.

But there was a big problem, and it was to do with his size. The Giant looked down at his giant boots and he could see that each boot was wider and bigger than the roads below.

This was no place to meet somebody like him. No place to live. He opened his giant mouth and bellowed.

The tiny people ran out of their houses and looked up at the Giant. He was as tall as an oak tree. His hair was as black as a starless night. His head was the size of a house.

He looked enormous.

The tiny people were terrified. They cried. They screamed. They shouted.

'Go away, you're too big to live here. Go away, we don't want you!'

This made the Giant very angry. He stamped his boots, and the ground shook violently and all the roofs fell off the houses.

The tiny villagers had to run and hide. One little boy stepped out onto the road and shouted up at the Giant, 'Go away! Look what you have done to our village. You simply don't fit in here!'

There was silence.

The people peeked out nervously to see what the Giant would do. To their surprise, he stopped stamping and shouting and quietly walked away.

The people came out from their hiding places.

'The roof has come off my house,' said the doctor.

'The windows are all broken in mine!' said the baker.

'My shop is ruined!' said the greengrocer.

'My bed is in pieces!' said the little boy. 'That Giant can't get away with this!'

'That's true,' said the boy's mother, 'but first we have to catch him.'

'How can we do that?' asked the little boy.

'We can write about him in the newspaper,' said his teacher.

So a newspaper reporter came to the village and asked lots of questions.

'What does he look like?'

'How big is the Giant?'

'What was he wearing?'

'What did he do?'

'How do you feel about what the Giant has done?'

The next day the newspaper printed the headline 'Help Catch the Giant', with a report about what had happened.

The Daily Nosepaper

DATE: *Sunny Day*

PRICE: *3 Beans*

HELP CATCH THE GIANT

HAVE YOU SEEN HIM?

Giant causes destruction to the village of Somewhere!

Yesterday, a Giant was seen terrorising the people in the village of Somewhere.

'He tore fences into the air as if they were made of spaghetti!' said the baker.

'He stamped his feet and the roof flew off my house,' said the doctor.

'My bed is in pieces,' said a boy from the village. These are just a few examples of the damage he caused, and the police are asking for everyone to be on the alert and contact the police station on: Somewhere 234

Here is a description of the Giant:

He is as tall as an oak tree.
His hair is as black as a starless night.
His head is the size of a house.
He looks enormous.

The next day, the police came asking questions to help the villagers catch this Giant. Then, a week later, the police had a meeting outside the Village Hall.

'We found that Giant, but we can't get him to talk,' the police chief declared.

Suddenly, a small voice cried out. It was the little boy. 'Hey Giant, what do you have to say for yourself?'

The Giant groaned, 'I've nothing to say!'

'Nothing!' shouted the baker.

'Nothing!' shouted the greengrocer.

'Nothing!' shouted the doctor.

'Nothing!' shouted all the villagers.

The little boy crept up to the Giant and asked, 'Why did you do it?'

The Giant groaned, 'I'm lonely. I was looking for Somewhere to live.'

'Where do you come from?' asked the boy.

'I come from Nowhere,' moaned the Giant.

'I see, but that doesn't mean you can trash our village,' said the boy.

'I didn't mean to,' mumbled the Giant. 'It's because I am too big.
I don't seem to fit in anywhere.'

The next day, the Giant was taken to the field to be judged for his crimes. Twelve chairs were placed facing the Giant. These were for the jurors. They had to listen to all the evidence and decide if the giant was guilty, or not guilty.

The 'judge', a local farmer, climbed into the digger arm of a tractor and shouted through a megaphone, 'Let the hearing begin!'

The teacher, who was acting as the prosecutor and putting the case against the Giant, stepped forward, took a deep breath and shouted, 'I call the following witnesses!'

'The roof came off my house!' shouted the doctor.

'All my windows are broken!' shouted the baker.

'My shop is ruined!' shouted the greengrocer.

'My bed is in pieces because of the Giant!' shouted the little boy.

'Do you admit to causing the damage to this village?' the teacher shouted up to the Giant.

'I do,' replied the Giant as softly as he could.

'Then can you explain to us why you did what you did?'

The Giant simply shrugged his shoulders. There was an awkward silence. Suddenly a small voice cried out. It was the little boy.

'I will – I know why he did it! He was angry. He's too big. Anyone can see that if they have eyes in their heads. He was looking for somewhere to live.'

'Where do you come from?' shouted the teacher.

'From Nowhere,' replied the Giant sadly.

A great sigh rang around the field.

'Put him in prison and throw away the key!' screamed the baker.

'Hear, hear!' shouted the people.

The judge then asked the jury, 'Have you reached a verdict?'

'We have, your honour. He is definitely guilty,' announced the foreman of the jury.

The Giant sighed. And the little boy cried out, 'But what use would it be to lock him away? What good would it do?'

'I agree,' shouted the judge, and he turned to the Giant. 'I am going to give you a community sentence.'

He held up a list for all to see.

'And you can live in the field next to the forest,' said the judge. There was silence. The Giant scratched his head, 'You mean I can live here even though I'm not the same size as all of you?'

'You can, but you must work for your living,' replied the judge.

Well, the Giant kept his word. He worked from morning till night, and when he had fixed all the damage, he began to build new houses and even made toys for the children. He was, it seemed, a truly clever Giant, even though he came from Nowhere.

But despite having found Somewhere to live, he never smiled, he never laughed and he hardly spoke.

The little boy could see that this Giant was lonely. What could be done?

The teacher had a really good idea.

'Let's put an advertisement in the newspaper in the Lonely Hearts section.'

'What do we need to write?' asked the little boy.

'Well, we need to describe our Giant, but we must write it as if he has written it.'

'You mean like this?' smiled the little boy. 'I am a Giant. I am one oak tree tall and I am very strong.'

'Yes, exactly like that,' said the teacher.

So they put the advertisement in the local newspaper.

The Daily Nosepaper

DATE:
Sunny Day

PRICE:
3 Beans

LONELY HEARTS

I am a Giant and I am one oak tree tall.

I have blue eyes and black hair.

I am as old as I feel, which is about the age of a young oak tree.

That's about 50 human years: not at all old for a Giant.

Hobbies:

I love making things. I can build houses and barns.

Recently I have been making toys for children.

I love children because generally they are really nice to me.

I am looking for a friend, someone who is kind and gentle and who has a sense of humour.

I have a home now in the field next to the forest in Somewhere, which is my address if you want to write to me and tell me about yourself.

The little boy was the first to spot the postman. His bike wobbled dangerously because his postbag was bulging with letters! Giant letters!

'Giant!' shouted the postman. 'You have some post!'

The Giant knelt down. 'Post? For me?'

'Yes,' shouted the postman, 'they must be from your friends.'

'But I don't have any friends.'

'Here, take them,' shouted the postman and cycled off into the distance.

'Open them!' shouted the little boy.

'But I don't understand,' frowned the Giant.

The little boy explained what he and the teacher had
done. The Giant was speechless, for nobody had ever
cared about how lonely he was.

'Open them!' the little boy shouted again.
The Giant shook his head sadly.
'What's up?' asked the little boy.
'I can't read,' admitted the Giant.
'I'll read them for you,' said the little boy.

One letter caught the Giant's
attention. 'I like the sound of her,'
he said, 'but...'

'I know,' said the little boy, 'but I
can write a letter for you.'

From the Giant
The field next to the forest.
Somewhere

Today

Dear Giantess,

You sound like just the kind of friend I would love to meet. And you are just the right size for me.

We seem to have so much in common. You say you love making things and maybe we could make things together.

I would like you to see the house I've built. It is strong but very simple and could do with a Giantess's touch.

If you would like to meet up, come to the field next to the forest by the village of Somewhere tomorrow.

I'll be waiting.
From, the Giant

The Giantess came to see the Giant in his field next to the forest.
It was *love* at first sight!

Now the Giant smiled and laughed.

'What has come over our Giant?' asked the people.

'He's in *love*,' laughed the little boy.

And where there is true *love*, a certain question usually follows: 'Will you marry me?'

And the Giantess shouted, 'Yes!' and everyone heard it for miles around.

The little boy wrote all the wedding invitations and the Giantess wrote a wedding list.

Wedding Invitation

The Giant and the Giantess invite you

To: Their wedding

On: Sunday

From: One o'clock in the afternoon

Place: In the field next to the forest in the village of Somewhere

Please reply to: The Giant and Giantess,
the field next to the forest, Somewhere

Wedding List

Beer barrels — to make into cups

Garden forks — to use for cutlery

Shovels or spades — to use as spoons

Old carts — to use as boxes for storage

An old bathtub — to use as a mixing bowl for cooking

Any old wheels — to make all sorts of gadgets,
like sewing machines and clocks

Trees blown down by the wind — to
make furniture out of the timber

All the people came to the wedding dressed up in their best clothes. The vicar shouted up at the Giant, 'What is your name?'

The Giant frowned. 'Name? I don't think I had a name. I wasn't anybody in Nowhere, but here I do feel like I'm Somebody.'

'I've got a name for you,' shouted the little boy, 'Sam Boady! Whenever you hear your name, you'll know you're truly Somebody!'

'Sam Boady it is then,' grinned the Giant.

'And my name is Riana,' smiled the Giantess.

'Do you, Sam Boady, take Riana for your wife?' asked the vicar.

'I certainly do,' grinned Sam Boady the Giant.

'And do you, Riana, take Sam Boady for your husband?'

'Try and stop me,' she laughed. Then, calming herself, she replied, 'I do.'

Then they had a party. Everyone danced and ate until they were ready to burst.

Finally, the Giant stood up, raised a barrel and said, 'I am now Sam Boady and I belong to *Somewhere*, and for this I thank you all from the bottom of my heart.'

The little boy cried out, 'Three cheers for Mr and Mrs Boady!'

'Hip hip hurrah!' shouted the people.

And the Giant and the Giantess lived happily ever after in the field next to the forest by the village that is Somewhere, a long, long way from a place called Nowhere.

Would you like to help the Giant?

We have created some exciting resources to enable you to become involved in his story. All you have to do is go to www.jkp.com/voucher and use the code **KEYWYFE** and you will find templates for all of the following items:

- A blank newspaper to help find the Giant. You will learn to be a reporter!

- A blank police questionnaire, so that you can role play with a friend or helper. One of you could be a villager from Somewhere, and the other a policeman or woman, then you could swap roles.

- A blank Lonely Hearts column in the newspaper. You can write your own column, and make it as interesting as possible in order to attract lots of replies.

- A blank letter between the Giant and Giantess. Again, you could role play with a friend or helper and write letters to each other introducing yourself and telling each other what you look like and what you like doing.

- A wedding invitation that needs completing with a time, a date, a place and the names of the characters getting married.

- A wedding list for you to imagine what Giants and Giantesses might like – you'll have to think BIG.

And maybe you could think up more ideas to help the Giant.

The Giant from Nowhere

This story was originally created as a result of a six-week project in a primary school working with children 5 to 8 years of age and promotes interactive participation, whether it is used with a classroom of children or on a one-to-one basis. Key points that underline this project are as follows:

- The story helps develop social awareness, as the reader and the child can become directly involved in the problems the Giant and the villagers face.

- This in turn develops problem-solving skills, prompting questions such as 'How can we find the Giant?' and 'What can we do about him?'

- The story explores similarities and differences between people and habitats.

- The reader and the child are encouraged to help either the Giant or the villagers, and depending on an individual child's needs, this can be achieved either through drawing or writing, therefore extending narrative skills.

- There are beautifully drawn examples of advertisements, questionnaires, letters, invitations and other resources available to download, all aimed at encouraging the reader and child to participate and make their own examples in order to help characters in the story. These activities develop communication on many different levels and help extend language skills and vocabulary.

- The story will have taken the reader and the child on a journey with a Giant and the villagers of Somewhere, a journey that will end in a wonderful celebration of love and mutual respect.

Teaching resources

In the downloads, you will find a lesson plan pack by the author to give you some ideas for how to become involved in the lonely Giant's life and help him solve his problems.

About the author

Frances Dickens taught in Lambeth for over 18 years, specialising in art, drama, English as a second language and special educational needs. All the skills she acquired through drama studies in education and special educational needs contributed to her practice for inspiring and motivating children through storytelling, drama and role play. She also published *The Story Maker* and *The Story Maker Motivator*, books designed to motivate young people to write creatively.

About the illustrator

Peter Hudspith studied Illustration and Design at Kingston University in the early 1980s. On graduating, he developed a career in freelance illustration. He worked on several projects with publishers, including Hodder & Stoughton ELT, Longman Books and Oxford University Press. He has worked with academic establishments including University College London, producing multiple illustrations to be used in child psycho-linguistic research. He now lives in Leeds where he has been working on portraits of famous artists.